ABEL'S ISLAND

DATE DUE

ABEL'S ISLAND ∘ *William Steig*

A Sunburst Book / *Farrar, Straus and Giroux*

For Jeanne

ABEL'S ISLAND

○1○

Early in August 1907, the first year of their marriage, Abel and Amanda went to picnic in the woods some distance from the town where they lived. The sky was overcast, but Abel didn't think it would be so inconsiderate as to rain when he and his lovely wife were in the mood for an outing.

They enjoyed a pleasant lunch in the sunless woods, sharing delicate sandwiches of pot cheese and watercress, along with hard-boiled quail egg, onions, olives, and black caviar. They toasted each other, and everything else, with a bright champagne which was kept cool in a bucket of ice. Then they played a jolly game of croquet, laughing without much reason, and they continued laughing as they relaxed on a carpet of moss.

When this happy nonsense got boring, Amanda crawled under a fern to read and Abel went off by himself for a bit. Roaming among the trees, admiring the verdure, he saw a crowd of daisies clustered above him, like gigantic stars, and decided to cut one down and present his wife with a pretty parasol.

He was already smiling at the little joke he would make as he held it over her head. He chose a perfect daisy and, using his handkerchief to avoid being soiled by the sap, carefully cut through the stem with his penknife.

The daisy over his shoulder, he sallied back toward his wife, very pleased with himself. It grew windy rather suddenly, and some rain fell, wherever it could through the foliage. It was hard to hold on to the flower.

His wife was under the fern exactly where he'd left her, absorbed in the life of her book. "I have something for you," he said, lifting the tip of the fern. Amanda looked up at him with large, puzzled eyes, as if a page of words had unaccountably turned into her husband. A sharp gust of wind tore the daisy from his grasp.

"It's raining," Amanda observed.

"Indeed it is!" said Abel indignantly as the rain fell

harder. It flailed down while they tried to gather their things. They huddled under Abel's jacket, he offended at the thoughtless weather, she worried, both hoping the downpour would soon let up. It didn't. It grew worse.

Tired of waiting, and of wondering where all that water came from, they decided to make a break for it. With the jacket over them, they headed for home, leaving their picnic behind, but they could make little progress against the wind. There was some angry thunder and dazzling flares of lightning near and far. "Dear one," cried Abel, "we must find shelter! Anywhere!" They stopped bucking the wind and ran skeltering with it, in dismay.

Clinging together, they ran, or were blown, through the woods, and eventually came up against a great, rocky cliff that shimmered in the pounding rain. They could be blown no farther.

The shelter they'd been seeking was very close. "Up here!" some voices called. "Up here!" Abel and Amanda looked up. Not far above them was the opening of a cave from which various furry faces peered out. They clambered together up into the cave, greatly relieved and panting for breath.

° 2 °

The cave was full of chattering animals who'd been lucky enough to find this haven. There were several mice that Abel and Amanda knew, and a family of toads they had once met at a carnival; all the rest were strangers. A weasel was off by himself in a corner, saying his prayers over and over.

Abel and Amanda were welcomed by all, and congratulations passed around. The storm raged as if it had lost its mind completely. The damp occupants of the cave stood close together in the vaulted entrance like actors who had played their parts and could now watch the rest of the show from the wings. The storm was turning into a full-fledged, screaming hurricane. Huge trees were bent by furious blasts of wind, branches broke, thunder volleyed, and crazy shafts of lightning zigzagged in the dark, steamy sky.

Abel and Amanda stood in the forefront of the group, entranced by the fearsome drama. Amanda craned forward to watch an oak topple, when suddenly the wind tore from her neck the scarf of gauze she was wearing, and this airy web of stuff flew like a ghost from the mouth of the cave. Abel gawked in horror, as if Amanda herself had been rudely snatched away.

He dashed out impulsively. To no avail, Amanda tried to stop him. "Abelard!" she screamed. She always used his full name when she thought he was acting foolish. He slid, unheeding, down the slope of rock.

The scarf hooked onto a bramble, from which he retrieved it, but when he tried to climb back with his trophy, the wind walloped and sent him spinning like weightless tumbleweed, his sweetheart's scarf in his paw. Helpless, unable even to struggle, he tucked in his head and was whirled along, shocked and bewildered.

Heaven knows how far he was hustled in this manner, or how many rocks he caromed off on his way. He did no thinking. He only knew it was dark and windy and wet, and that he was being knocked about in a world

that had lost its manners, in a direction, as far as he could tell, not north, south, east, or west, but whatever way the wind had a mind to go; and all he could do was wait and learn what its whims were.

Its whim was to fling him against a huge nail, where he fastened with all his strength. The nail was stuck in a fragment of board that had once been part of a large animal's house, and the fragment of board was embedded in a gully full of gravel. Abel clung to the nail and to Amanda's scarf, fighting the wind, whose force seemed to increase when he stopped riding with it.

The torrent of wet air tearing past made breathing difficult. Abel stuffed Amanda's scarf into his inner pocket and buried his head under his blazer. He soon found himself haunch-deep in a swelling stream. Rain had filled the gully and a heavy flow of muddy water loosened his board from its gravel mooring. He went sailing along, spinning this way and that, drilled with a trillion bullets of rain. Whatever happened no longer surprised him. It was all as familiar as one's very worst dreams.

It was definitely night now. He could see nothing, not his own paw in front of his face, but he knew he was moving swiftly upon his board. Soon he sensed he was in a river. In the immense darkness he could hear only wind and, all around him, rain falling into water.

A new sound slowly emerged, the murmur of roiling foam. His boat was moving toward it, and it rose to a turbulent roar. Then, with no advance notice, the boat tilted vertically and shot downward on what he was sure was a waterfall. Plunged deep in the water below, he fought against drowning; then, still hugging his nail, he rose slowly into a maelstrom of churning river, gasping for indrafts of air. Never had he been subjected to such rude treatment. How long could it last? How long, he wondered, could he abide it?

As if to answer that question, his craft shot forward again and he was pitched, jerked, and bandied about by the writhing, charging stream. His boat capsized, then righted itself and began turning over and over; each time his exasperated head bobbed up, he gasped for his possibly final breath. His fortitude amazed him.

Suddenly, thump! He was no longer moving. His craft had struck an unyielding mass and stuck in it. He had no idea, in the blackness, where in the world he was— it was any wet, windy where. He could feel the heavy water hurrying past him, tugging at his clothes. Drenched, cold, exhausted, he still held on to his nail, but the water pressing him against it allowed him to ease his grip, and it was a relief.

The wind still screamed, the rain still pelted, the river still raged, but he felt in some sort of harbor. Momentarily moored, wherever it was, he was able to wonder about Amanda. She was surely safe in the cave, among friends. She would be worrying about him, of course, but he would be getting back to her as soon as

he could. This was the weirdest experience of his life. He could never forget it. Never forget it . . . never forget . . . But for the moment he did. Merciful sleep shrouded his senses.

He slept curled around the rusty nail, wind and rain drubbing his tired young body.

° 3 °

Abel slept for fourteen hours. When his eyes opened, he was startled to find he was not where he ought to be; that is, in bed with his wife, Amanda. There was no wife; there were no walls. There was only a dazzling brightness in a landscape such as he had never seen. It was midafternoon.

As always after a hurricane, the atmosphere was crystal clear. He was now able to see his boat, the piece of board with the rusty nail that had probably saved his life. It was lodged in the uppermost branches of a tree that was mainly submerged in the river. Above was an endless cerulean blue. Below, water flowed swiftly, sparkling like champagne in the sun. The water was all around him, but some distance to his left, and some distance to his right, more trees stuck up out of the water, and beyond the trees on both sides the ground rose into wooded hills. Turning around, he saw behind him the waterfall over which he had plunged.

His tree seemed to be in the middle of the river. There was no doubt he was on an island. The rain must have ended shortly after he fell asleep, and during that time the flood had crested. It had already subsided some, or else he would not be as far above the water as he was. He would be able to descend to solid ground when the river fell farther.

He stood up, stretching, and winced; all his muscles ached. He had to sit down again. He wished Amanda was with him, or, better yet, he with her. As far as he could tell, apart from the trees, he was the only living thing between the horizons. He let out his loudest "Halloo-oo-oo-oo," then listened. There was no response, not even an echo.

The state of his clothes disturbed him. Damp and lumpy, they no longer had style. That would be corrected as soon as possible. He stared into the distance and speculated. "They're all wondering where I am, of course. Many I don't even know are wondering. It's certainly gotten around that Abelard Hassam di Chirico Flint, of the Mossville Flints, is missing."

It was distressing to consider the misery and anxiety his absence was causing those who cared. Search parties were surely out, but they wouldn't be anywhere near him. How could they even begin to guess what had happened: that, by freak chance, rain had formed a rivulet around a sort of boat he had boarded accidentally, that the rivulet, swelling, had taken him into a stream, the

stream had carried him into a river, the river had rushed him over a waterfall, and that he was now where he was, on his boat at the top of a tree, on an island, in whatever river this was.

When the water subsided, he would descend and go home—and what a story he'd have to tell! Meanwhile, he wished he had something to eat—a mushroom omelet, for example, with buttered garlic toast. Being hungry in addition to being marooned like this was really a bit too much. Absent-mindedly, he nibbled at a twig on his branch. Ah, cherry birch! One of his favorite flavors. The familiar taste made him feel a little more at home on his roost in the middle of nowhere.

He munched on the bark of a tender green shoot, his cheek filled with the pulp and the juice. He was eating. He sat there, vaguely smug, convinced that he had the strength, the courage, and the intelligence to survive. His eyes glazed over and he returned to sleep.

° 4 °

Abel awoke early in the morning, a new mouse after his second spell of healing slumber. Stretching felt good. It struck him that his landscape had changed. There were trees in his vicinity, all around him. His boat had been stopped by a towering one near the river's edge.

Looking below, he saw that his tree towered not only

because it was tall but because it stood on a rocky prominence. The water had returned to its proper level. In many places the grass was flattened, half buried in silt and gravel. Otherwise, it seemed a normal world.

He climbed to the very top of his tree and made a survey. He was indeed on an island. He could see the waterfall and river above; he was on one side of the island, by one fork of the river, and through the trees he could make out the fork on the opposite side; way below, he could see where the two forks rejoined. No one was anywhere visible.

It was time to be getting home. He started descending the birch, and in another moment he was grinning like an idiot. He was climbing down a tree he had never climbed up! Amanda would enjoy hearing about this. She had a sense of humor almost as sharp as his.

How good to be standing on solid earth again. He did some quick knee bends and ran around the tree just for the joy of the free movement. Then he sat on a stone, his elbows on his knees, and looked up and down the river. Perhaps by now they had managed to figure out what had happened to him and would be turning up in a boat, or something, after all. He waited, and to keep himself amused, he hummed snatches of his favorite cantata and imagined how he would narrate his adventures. He would be quite matter-of-fact, especially about the parts where he had shown courage and endurance; he would leave the staring and gasping to his audience.

No one turned up and Abel realized he'd been expecting too much. They'd never look for him here. Well, he would have to cross the river, one way or another. He ran to the other side of the island; perhaps the river was narrower there. It was wider. He ran back. He removed his shoes and socks, rolled up his trousers, and waded into the water to try the current.

No, it would be impossible to reach the far shore by swimming, even though he was a competent swimmer. The rush of water was much too strong. He'd be dashed against a rock, or dragged under and drowned.

He needed a boat of some sort. How about his board and nail? Perhaps he could do something with that. He climbed his tree, dislodged the board, and followed it down when it fell to the ground. He stood over it muttering to himself, thoughtfully fingering a filament of his mustache. How could he navigate this crude piece of wood? With a rudder! If he held the rudder at an acute angle, the boat would gradually work its way to the opposite shore. That would be bending the power of the stream to his own ends.

With a stick he scratched a diagram in the sand. It was a long rectangle, the river, crossed by a long diagonal, the course his boat would take. He should eventually land on the other side, much farther downstream. He was pleased with the way his mind was working.

He managed to tear a flat strip of wood from a nearby log and with his pearl-handled penknife whittled a shapely handle. The nail would help him keep the rudder firmly in position. Now he put on his shoes and socks, arranged his clothes as neatly as he could, and edged his boat into the water. It was really much too long since he'd seen Amanda. Since their wedding they had not been apart for as much as a day.

He got aboard, pushed off from the shore with his rudder, and quickly braced it against the nail, holding the handle firmly in his paws. The rudder worked! He was moving away from the bank. Then the boat reached the powerful current farther out. It began to bobble and buck. Abel's rudder shuddered in his paws, though he used all his strength to hold it steady. His knees bobbled and bucked with the boat as it sped along, snaking its way in the writhing grooves of the stream. It pitched left, then right, then the rudder was wrenched from his grasp; and now he was no longer a helmsman but a stunned passenger on a bit of flotsam at the mercy of the rampaging water.

His boat skedaddled up to a rock, hit it catty-cornered, and spun, and Abel was suddenly in the water, without his boat, borne along like a limp rag.

By good fortune, instead of being carried past the island and down the river, he was able to catch hold of a low-hanging streamer of weeping willow and pull himself ashore. The whole ordeal had lasted just a minute.

He ambled back to his starting point near the cherry birch, his toes turned awkwardly in. The mess of wet clothes he wore added to his sense of ineptitude and shame; he was used to their being dry and pressed. Where had he erred, he wondered. He should have bound the rudder to the nail, of course. He had been too hasty in his preparations, and he had underestimated the force of the rapids.

He would have to design and build a real boat, not a raft like the piece of board that had just quit his company. Perhaps it should be a sailboat; his jacket might serve as a sail. The rudder this time would be firmly secured through a hole in the stern.

The sailboat so clearly envisioned, some confidence returned. He felt a bit proud, even in his wet pants. He found a piece of driftwood, somewhat disgusting since it had been gnawed and bored and channeled by lower forms of life. But he couldn't afford to be overly sensitive now. He dragged the driftwood to the edge of the water. It would be the bottom of his boat. He washed his paws.

Next he peeled three large sections of bark from a dead tree, and shaped them for the sides by bending and breaking them on the straight edge of a rock. He collected a great deal of tough grass and fashioned lengths of rope by tying the ends together. When he thought he had enough of this rope, he began cutting grooves in the driftwood.

It was slow work with the small penknife. Not thinking, he fell to using his teeth. What? He drew back for a moment, in revulsion. Then he continued to gnaw away. He had never before gnawed on anything but food. But the grooves were done in no time, and he didn't honestly mind the taste of the somewhat decayed wood.

He fitted the bark into the grooves and then went to work lashing everything together, going round and round with the rope, and over and under, until his boat could hardly be seen for what it really was under all the lashings. Now he gathered a heap of soft grass and, with stone and stick for hammer and chisel, tamped it into all the crevices to prevent leakage.

He was pleased with his ingenuity. He had never

built a boat before; in fact, though he was a married mouse, he had never built anything, or done a day's work. However, he had watched others working, so ideas came to him readily. When he finished his caulking, he made a mast with a crosspiece, or boom, out of branches.

The mast was inserted among the numerous lashings and fastened with more. He made a rudder like the first, put it through a hole in the stern as he had planned, and surveyed the completed boat. Considering the crude materials and the lack of tools, he had to admit it was a fine piece of work. Too bad the bright day was his only witness.

Before dressing the mast with his jacket, where it hung like a scarecrow's slack raiment, he removed from the inner pocket Amanda's scarf, the bit of beloved gauze that accounted for his being where he was. He kissed the piece of fluff and tucked it inside his shirt.

A favorable breeze was drifting across the island toward the shore opposite. It seemed a good omen. He looked back in a farewell glance at this remote part of the world's geography that had given him shelter for two nights. Then he shoved his ship into the water and leaped aboard, grabbing the tail of his coat with one paw, the rudder with the other.

Boat number two fared worse than the first. The stream was too swift and the breeze too light for the sail to be effective. The boat swung around despite the rudder, hit a rock, and shattered. Luckily, Abel was pitched into a pebbled shallow and managed to scramble ashore, where he stood and watched his jacket and the wreck of his ship go the way of the river.

Wringing his clothes, he made his way back to the birch, which had become his center of operations. He resented the stream and meant to best it.

Abel grimly decided that in his next effort he would not count on a rudder; rudders were too dependent on the behavior of wayward water. Nor would he count on a sail, because wind was fickle. He would rely only on the strength of his own two arms. He had seen water striders, those insects that support themselves in swift streams on long legs kept wide apart. He would build a sort of water strider, a catamaran, and row it.

Excited by this new idea, he quickly put together a catamaran of crisscross sticks in the form of a pyramid, tying the sticks together wherever they crossed. Next, using that remarkable, newly discovered tool, his rodent teeth, he made two long oars, or sweeps, which he placed in notches he had gnawed out for oarlocks. In a sporting spirit, he tied his handkerchief to the top of a pole as a pennant.

Convinced he had finally solved the problem of conquering the stream, he launched his craft and climbed into the captain's seat with his oars. The moment they touched the water, they were wrenched from his grasp, and the river took over once more. Once more he foundered on a rock, and once more barely managed to

scramble back up on the island.

He was beginning to feel he owed his wife, and the whole world, an explanation. He wished he could let them all know what was delaying him.

° 5 °

He sat on a stone, staining it with his wetness. He pulled at his snout and chewed his lips. He was beginning to comprehend the awkwardness of his position.

He was marooned on an island, nowhere near civilization, as far as he could tell; and if he was going to get off, it must be by his own devices. But he was obviously not going to cross that river in any boat he could put together out of the available materials.

He had worked so quickly that it was still only mid-afternoon. He returned to the birch, thoughtfully munching on mushrooms along the way. He knew which ones were safe. He had studied mushrooms in Souris's *Botany* at home, and he and Amanda had picked them in the forest. He was hungrier than he had realized.

Abel posed this question to himself: Other than by swimming or on boats, how *do* rivers get crossed? By tunnels and bridges, of course. Could he tunnel under that river with his paws, his penknife, and a homemade wooden shovel perhaps; no pickax, no crowbar, no wheelbarrow or wagon, not even a pail to carry out the earth and rocks?

He would have to start far back from the shore, so as not to have to carry the diggings out of too vertical a shaft; and he would have to burrow way down deep where it was almost as hard as rock, if indeed it wasn't rock itself. And how could he be sure he was tunneling well under the riverbed? What if the river flooded his tunnel, or if the tunnel simply collapsed on him? What a way that would be for the descendant of an ancient and noble family to die! Pressed out of existence in mundane mud, and no one even knowing what had happened to him, or where. Only he himself would know, and just

for a second at that. The tunnel idea was out.

He would have to construct a bridge of some sort. He was intelligent and had imagination. Something would surely occur to him. The situation was by no means hopeless. However, he was clearly not leaving the island that day. He decided to explore it.

His birch was situated near the upper end, which he had already hastily crossed. He now carefully walked its length. It was a typical piece of the temperate zone, with familiar kinds of rocks, trees, bushes, brambles, grass, and other plants. It was gravelly near the water, rockiest at the lower end, and, from a mouse's point of view, hilly. Abel estimated the island to be about 12,000 tails long, 5,000 wide.

What most felt like home in this strange place full of familiar objects was the birch. He had already slept in it twice. Returning there, he heard birdsong and saw birds, but they showed no interest in him, and he felt no hope of communicating with them. They were wild, and he civilized. He knew that certain pigeons could be taught to carry messages. He had heard the woeful sounds of a mourning dove, but that was the wrong kind of pigeon.

Though he was having a most extraordinary experience, Abel was bored. It was not an adventure of his choosing. It was being foisted on him, and that he resented. He even began to dislike his friends back home for lacking the powers of logic to puzzle out where he was so they could come to his rescue. He wished to be in his own home, with his loving wife, surrounded by the books he liked to browse in, by his paintings and his elegant possessions, dressed in neat modish clothes, comfortable in a stuffed chair. He wouldn't even mind being bored *there,* staring at the patterns in the wallpaper. He was fed up with the stupid, pointless island.

But the stupid island was where he was going to spend this night, at least, in soiled clothes that were beginning to smell fusty. What if he had to stay longer than this night? Food would be no problem. The island abounded with edible plants, many of which he recognized from illustrations in his encyclopedia. And there were insects he could eat if it came to a choice of that or starving. He could continue to sleep in the birch, where, if not completely protected, he had the advantage of a high redoubt, the upper hand in case of a conflict.

For dinner he ate wild carrots, carefully scraped with his knife. Then, with his paws folded across his belly, where the nourishment was being extracted from the carrots, he sat under his birch in the opal glow of the waning day and took stock of his resources. He had a shirt, trousers, socks, shoes, underwear, a necktie, and suspenders. His jacket had gone with the smashed sailboat, his handkerchief with the catamaran. In his pockets he had the stub of a pencil, a small scratch pad, quite damp, a few coins, the keys to his house, and his penknife.

And of course there was Amanda's scarf. He pressed it to his face. In spite of all the washings it had been through, its threads still held Amanda's dear scent. Abel fought off a wave of self-pity. Only when he considered the unhappiness he was causing Amanda, his family, his friends, did he finally allow himself some hot tears. Despair was darkening his spirit. Deep down, where truth dwells, he wasn't at all sure he'd be getting off the island soon.

He rested against his tree and gazed at the river just being itself, burbling along. The river was where it

ought to be; Abel wasn't. He felt out of place. When it grew dark, he climbed to the top of his tree and lay down in the crook of a branch, hugging Amanda's scarf.

He was suddenly thrilled to see his private, personal star arise in the east. This was a particular star his nanny had chosen for him when he was a child. As a child, he would sometimes talk to this star, but only when he was his most serious, real self, and not being any sort of a show-off or clown. As he grew up, the practice had somehow worn off.

He looked up at his old friend as if to say, "You see my predicament."

The star seemed to respond, "I see."

Abel next put the question: "What shall I do?"

The star seemed to answer, "You will do what you will do." For some reason this reply strengthened Abel's belief in himself. Sleep gently enfolded him. The constellations proceeded across the hushed heavens as if tiptoeing past the dreaming mouse on his high branch.

Abel dreamed of Amanda—odd, unfinished dreams. As the new day dawned, he dreamed he was falling. There was nothing to get hold of in the awesome void, and he plummeted toward unthinkable pain on the hard ground. Was he really dreaming? Yes. But he was also really falling. Dream and reality were the same. He hit a leafy branch which broke his fall and he landed in deep grass and was awake. It sickened him to see the river in the pale, early light.

° 6 °

Was it just an accident that he was here on this unin-
habited island? Abel began to wonder. Was he being
singled out for some reason; was he being tested? If so,
why? Didn't it prove his worth that such a one as
Amanda loved him?

Did it? Why *did* Amanda love him? He wasn't all that
handsome, was he? And he had no particular accomp-
lishments. What sort of mouse was he? Wasn't he really
a snob, and a fop, and frivolous on serious occasions, as
she had once told him during a quarrel? He had acted
silly even at his own wedding, grinning during the
solemnities, clowning when cutting the cake. What made
him act that way when he did?

Full of such questions, he went to wash his face in the
river that kept him captive, and drank some of its water.
It was foolish, he realized, to harbor a grudge toward this
river. It had no grudge against him. It happened to be
where it was; it had probably been there for eons.

He found a bush of ripe raspberries and ate his fill
for breakfast. This was his third morning on the island.
Carefully cracking the few seeds that remained in his
mouth, he thought again about a bridge. He decided he
could make one of rope, a single floating strand on which
he could pull himself across. It would have to be strong
enough so the current wouldn't tear it, and light enough

so he could sling it across to the other side. He would tie
a stone on one end and try to make it catch in some
bushes he'd picked out on the far shore.

This time he proceeded methodically, not in nervous
haste. He went first to defecate, behind a rock, though
no one was watching. Then he cut long blades of tough
crab grass, and sat cross-legged on the ground tearing
the grass lengthwise so that each blade became many
strands. He worked this way for hours and he enjoyed
the absorbing task.

When he felt he had enough, he proceeded to braid
and weave the long fibers to form a continuous rope. Occasionally he would encircle the rope with a few strands
of grass and tie a firm knot to prevent unraveling. He
was doing the kind of thing he had often, leaning on
his cane, watched others do.

Noon passed. His thoughts concerned only rope—its
making and how he would use it. But as the rope grew,
Amanda, who was always somewhere in his mind, came
forward. What was she thinking, he wondered.

No doubt they had searched for him in a large area
around the cave, dreading to find him injured, or dead.
But what did they make of not finding him at all? Had
they gone after him right away? The hurricane would
have prevented them from getting very far. He was certain Amanda had to be restrained from risking her life
to aid him. They must have spent a sleepless night inside
the cave and started looking early in the morning when

the storm was over. By now the whole town was certainly looking; his powerful father would have seen to that. They might look pretty far. But this far? Never!

How frantic Amanda must be! But so much greater her joy when she had him back again.

It was evening when he'd woven enough rope to span the river. He had it neatly coiled on the ground in a large ring. It would be wise to wait for morning, though, before crossing over. If he crossed now, he'd have to sleep on the other side, where he'd be less at home than he was here. And he was tired.

He ate the seed from the grass he'd worked with; it was scattered all around him. He drank at the river and then, for diversion, wandered toward the interior of the island, chewing on fragrant raspberries as he wandered. In a pleasant place, open yet sheltered by overhanging boughs, the hollow bole of a dead tree lay on the ground. He entered.

Recalling his fall from the birch, he felt this log would afford a safer night's lodging. He went to work carting out some of the rot. The log had limbs which were also hollowed by decay. It amounted to a house with several wings. No beast of prey could fit into that log, or reach beak, talon, fang, or claw deep enough to get at Abel where he planned to sleep. As for snakes, there were stones with which to close the entrance when he went in.

He lay on his back for a while, Amanda's scarf held with both paws to his breast. Having worked all day,

seriously and well, he was warmed with a proper self-regard. He had provided food and shelter for himself, and woven a rope which would be his bridge to freedom, home, and love.

He spent that night in the log, eager for the morning. He believed he could shoot his rope across the river by using his suspenders as a slingshot.

◦ 7 ◦

At sunrise Abel was at the river, where he washed, had breakfast, and got to work on his bridge. He set up his suspenders as a slingshot, fastening one end to a stout bush. Then he arranged his rope in a few long, loose loops that would straighten out easily as it arched over the gap. He tied one end to a stone and the other to the bush, made a pocket in the suspenders to hold the stone, and was ready for his shot.

Grasping the stone in its pocket and leaning backward, he pulled mightily, stretching the suspenders as far as the elastic would allow, and aimed his bridge, or life line, in the direction of the bushes on the opposite shore. Fervently hoping for success, he released his hold.

The stone, with the rope trailing it, made a small parabola in the air, and the line, as if with a sigh, fell limply into the river only ninety tails away. He quickly hauled it in. A bit of faith still remaining, he set up his machinery and tried again, using a lighter stone. The result was even more disappointing. The rope was wet now, and heavy.

Abel tried swinging the stone around and around above his head with a gradually lengthening line and then releasing it like a bola. This simpler method

worked better than the suspenders, but not enough better to matter. He pulled in the rope and sat beside it, clutching his head in his paws.

The stubbornness of his character stood him now in good stead. He refused to consider himself defeated. A few minutes of gloomy pondering produced a new idea: a bridge of steppingstones. Why hadn't he thought of this simple scheme before? He would make piles of stones, using each pile as a step to build the next one, until he'd made enough to walk, or hop, his way across the river.

He spent the rest of the day amassing a huge heap of pebbles and rocks, going farther and farther afield to find them. By sundown he was so exhausted he lay down in his log without having eaten, and fell asleep before the birds had finished making their final evening statements.

The next morning, after wolfing a big breakfast, he stood in water up to his neck, building the first step. He viewed it with satisfaction. He realized that the steps would have to be close together, because he could make only a short leap carrying a heavy weight. He managed a second and a third step, and that was all.

The would-be fourth step, which was started in swifter water, never formed, because the current carried away the largest rocks Abel could handle. It was a hopeless project. The middle of the river, if ever he could reach it, was surely very deep, and even if the rocks held, the

amount required to make a single step would be more than he could find on the island or carry in what remained of his life.

He would keep thinking. It was his family tradition never to give up but to keep gnawing away until problems were solved. For the time being, however, he had run out of ideas. He began to develop an obstinate patience.

In the next few days he discovered additional sources of nourishment: groundnuts, mulberries, wild mustard, wild onions, new kinds of mushrooms, spearmint, peppermint, and milkweed. His former days of reading helped him identify these plants. He made a hammock of grass fibers and swung himself in it by pulling on a rope, swaying from side to side like seaweed on the rolling sea, full of vacant wonder. He was stunned with his own solitude, his own silence.

Every night he slept in the log. It had become half hotel, half home. But he still regarded the birch as the focal point of his comings and goings. He would often climb it to scan the surroundings and sit there chewing on a twig.

By the end of the month of August he knew he was an inhabitant of the island, whether he liked it or not. It was where he lived, just as a prison is where a prisoner lives. He thought constantly of Amanda. He thought of his parents, his brothers, sisters, friends. He knew they were grieving and he was moved by their grief. He, at least, knew he was alive. They didn't. What was Amanda doing? How did her days drag out? Did she still write poetry? Was she able to eat, to sleep, to enjoy her existence in any way?

Her image was in his mind, as clear as life sometimes, and he smiled with wistful tenderness, remembering her ways. Amanda was dreamy. It often seemed she was dreaming the real world around her, the things that were actually happening. She could dream Abel when he was right there by her side. Abel loved this dreaminess in her. He loved her dreamy eyes.

Wherever he went about the island, he wore Amanda's scarf around his neck, the ends tied in a knot. He would not leave it in the log.

∘8∘

It was September when Abel evolved another scheme for getting home. He would catapult himself across the stream. With his clothes stuffed full of grass for a cushioned landing, using a small stump as a winch, he tried with a rope to bend a sapling down to the ground so it could fling him over the water. But he managed to bend it only two and a half tails. That was all the wood yielded to his strength. So this scheme, too, miscarried.

A few days later he succeeded in making fire. He had

learned about the primitive methods in school, but he had never tried for himself. After a series of failures, he finally found the right kind of stick to twirl in the right piece of dry wood, and the right kind of tinder to flare with the first flame. His fires were as magical to him as they had been to his prehistoric ancestors.

He first used his fires for smoke beacons, to attract the attention of some civilized being who might just possibly be among the trees on the far shores. When he had a fire burning, he would partially cover it with damp leaves so that it sent up a thick white smoke.

He learned to roast his seeds by placing them on rocks close to the fire. Later he was able to cook various vegetables, flavored with wild garlic or onions, in pots made of a reddish clay from the lower end of the island. The clay was baked hard in prolonged, intense firing.

He also made paper-thin bowls of this clay, and from time to time he would float one down the river with a note in it, and a flower or sprig of grass sticking out to attract notice. One of his notes:

Whoever finds this: Please forward it to my wife, Amanda di Chirico Flint, 89 Bank Street, Mossville.

DEAREST ANGEL—I am ALIVE! I am alone on an island, marooned, somewhere above where this note will be found, God willing. There is a tall cherry birch on the northern end of the island. The island is about 12,000 tails long and is below a waterfall. Do not worry, but send help.

> My utmost and entire love,
>
> ABEL

Whoever finds this, please send help too. I will be able to give a substantial reward.

Sometimes Abel would climb to the top of his birch, or some other tree, and wave his white shirt up and down, and back and forth, for many minutes, hoping that someone would make a miraculous appearance, return his signal, and come to the rescue. There was no point in yelling; the river was too noisy for his halloos to carry.

During the equinoctial rains, he spent the whole of a dismal day indoors, listening to the unceasing downpour on the outside of his log, watching it through his door and through portholes he had made—the infinite pall of falling rain, the sagging, wet vegetation, the drops dripping from everything as if counting themselves, the runnels and pools, the misty distances—and feeling an ancient melancholy.

Rain caused one to reflect on the shadowed, more poignant parts of life—the inescapable sorrows, the speechless longings, the disappointments, the regrets, the cold miseries. It also allowed one the leisure to ponder questions unasked in the bustle of brighter days; and if one were snug under a sound roof, as Abel was, one felt somehow mothered, though mothers were nowhere around, and absolved of responsibilities. Abel had to cherish his dry log.

At night, when it cleared up, he went out in the wet grass and watched a young moon vanishing behind clouds and reappearing, over and over, like a swimmer out on the sea. Then he went inside the log, barred the entrance, and lay down with Amanda's scarf.

Drugged with the aroma of rotting wood, he lost consciousness. There was a din of crickets outside, and the pauseless roar of the river, and the stately world was illumined with pearly moonlight; but inside the log it was dark and hushed, like a crypt.

The castaway dreamed all night of Amanda. They were together again, in their home. But their home was not 89 Bank Street, in Mossville; it was a garden, something like the island, and full of flowers. What was marvelous about this otherwise ordinary dream was that Abel *knew* he was dreaming and was certain that his wife was dreaming the very same dream at the same time, so that they were as close to each other as they'd ever been in the solid world.

° 9 °

The feeling that he could visit Amanda in dreams haunted Abel. Perhaps he could reach her during his waking hours as well. He began sending her "mind messages." Sitting in the crotch of his favorite branch on the birch, he would project his thoughts, feelings, questions, yearnings, in what he considered the direction of his home. Sometimes he felt that Amanda could "hear" these messages and was responding with loving messages of her own. This feeling elated him.

He became convinced he could fly to his wife through the air, or glide, like a flying squirrel. He made a glider by stretching a catalpa leaf across two sticks, attached it to his back, and climbed to the top of his birch. From there he flung himself into the void, arms outstretched, aiming for the far shore. Instead of the soaring ride he had anticipated, he made a slow, graceful half circle, heels over head, and thudded down on his back in the grass. He lay there for several hours, brokenhearted and dazed with pain.

When body and spirits recovered, he took to climbing his birch again. One day, when he was winding his way upward, around and around the trunk, it seemed to him that the tree was somehow aware of his ascending spiral, and that it enjoyed his delicate scurryings, just as he enjoyed the rugged toughness and sensible architecture

of the tree. He felt the tree knew his feelings, though no words could pass between them.

He believed in his "visits" with Amanda; he had his birch, and his star, and the conviction grew in him that the earth and the sky knew he was there and also felt friendly; so he was not really alone, and not really entirely lonely. At times he'd be overcome by sudden ecstasy and prance about on high rocks, or skip along the limbs of trees, shouting meaningless syllables. He was, after all, in the prime of his life.

Late in September, when he woke up mornings, he would see rime on the ground. That and the nip in the air made him worry about the coming of winter. What if he was still there? In his tours of the island he had found acorns and hickory nuts and also wild sunflowers full of seed. He began storing these in his log.

Living in the heart of nature, he began to realize how much was going on in the seeming stillness. Plants grew and bore fruit, branches proliferated, buds became flowers, clouds formed in ever-new ways and patterns, colors changed. He felt a strong need to participate in the designing and arranging of things. The red clay from which he had fashioned pots and dishes inspired him to try his hand at making something just for its own sake, something beautiful.

He made a life-size statue of Amanda. Though it didn't really resemble her, it did look like a female mouse. He was amazed at what he had wrought. Good or bad, it was sculpture. It was art. He tried again and again, profiting from his mistakes, and finally he felt he had a likeness of his wife real enough to embrace.

Next he made statues of his dear, indulgent mother, from whose wealth his own income came, and of his various sisters and brothers, and he stood them all outside his log where he could see them from the windows.

Another day he did his father. Him he carved in tough wood, fiercely gnawing the forms out with his teeth. He stood back often to study the results of his gnawing, and

at last felt he had captured the proud, stern, aloof, strong, honest look of his male parent. He stood this statue next to that of his mother.

Abel had not been keeping track of the days, but the color of the leaves was being transformed from green to various yellows, burning golds, flaming reds, and he realized it was October. He gathered masses of fluff from the seed pods of milkweed to keep him warm in his log.

With threads of grass, he wove mats for his floor, and curtains for his windows to keep out drafts, and he tacked these curtains up with thorns. Later he made shutters out of bark.

He relayed the news of his doings to Amanda, sure that his airborne messages reached her. He added to his winter store of food, at what he thought was her urging, and meanwhile he kept dining on what remained available outdoors. At night, from its eminence, his star shone down on him with proud approval.

When the trees were in the full flame of autumn's fire, Abel wandered aimlessly over the island until the sight of the high color had him glowing inwardly with sensations of yellow, orange, and red. He pressed the juice from elderberries he had garnered earlier in the month and stored it in clay pots to let it turn to wine. His paws and shirt were stained with purple, but he no longer cared about his appearance.

In gray November, when the dry leaves huddled in drifts on the ground, he made a remarkable discovery. He thought he had thoroughly explored the island. He hadn't. Near the lower end, by the eastern shore, he found a huge watch with a chain, and an enormous book. The watch was as large as a dining table to accommodate three mice. The book was four tails long, three wide, and almost a tail thick. There was a stone on top of it, and it was the stone, no doubt, and the lay of the ground, that had kept it from being washed away in the flood.

Judging by its condition, the book had been there some time and had seen several changes of weather in addition to the flood. The cloth binding was puffed into blisters and wrinkled; the title, *Sons and Daughters*, was

faded and hard to discern. Some large creature had been on the island, perhaps picnicking, and had gone away forgetting the book and the watch. Probably the stone had been placed on the book to keep it from blowing open.

Abel's heart raced. The island was known to civilized

creatures and would be visited again! He would have to leave signs all about to make his presence known. Meanwhile, he was curious about the book. With great effort he rolled away the stone, which was larger than himself, and pried the stiff cover open.

The pages were buckled and water-stained, but the type was clear enough. He managed to separate the title page from page 1, and began reading, pacing from side to side on the printed lines. The book opened with the description of a masquerade ball. The characters were bears, which, like other large animals, had always fascinated Abel. It was wonderful to have a long book to entertain him and keep him company. He decided to read a chapter each day.

He closed the book and carefully buried it under a heap of leaves to prevent further damage by sun and rain. Then, with the end of the chain slung over his shoulder, he began hauling the watch to his house. It was heavy, but the smooth platinum of the case slid over the dry fallen leaves and made the hauling not too hard.

°10°

Early next morning Abel raced back to the book, removed the leaves, and took up reading where he had left off. The masked ball was a happy affair, even though there was talk among the guests of possible war. The main character was a captain in his country's army. He was snout over claws in love with a beautiful young lady bear with whom he danced a couple of waltzes. Abel had to laugh over one of the bears, who was masquerading as a mouse. What he read made him wistful for his normal life, but he still enjoyed reading.

After hopping from ide to side eagerly devouring the words, he forced himself to stop at the close of the chapter. He re-covered the book with the leaves and went home.

There, in case the bears who had left the book behind, or anyone else, should turn up, Abel made clay tablets like this:

and baked them in his fire.

The next day the signs were placed in well-chosen parts of the island, leaning against trees or stones, with the arrow always pointing to his home, the log. He had to drag the tablets along the ground with a rope, they were so large. He noted that there were thin wafers of ice along the shore, and for a moment he had excited visions of a frozen river that could be crossed by walking; but he quickly remembered that such swiftly flowing water could not freeze.

He was curious to know if the watch would run. Some prodding and shoving with a pole in the grooves of the stem-winder made it turn round a dozen times. The watch began to tick. The sounds he had become accustomed to, the roaring and gurgling of the river, the wailing and whining of the wind, the pattering and dripping of rain, the chirruping of birds and the chirring of insects, had natural, irregular rhythms, which were very soothing, but the steady, mechanical tempo of the watch gave him something he had been wanting in this wild place. It and the book helped him feel connected to the civilized world he'd come from. He had no use for the time the watch could tell, but he needed the ticking.

Abel led a busy life. He had used up the pages of his scratch pad floating messages down the river, but he still occasionally sent up smoke signals, and once in a while, futile as it seemed, he would climb a tree and wave his stained and tattered shirt. He had his book to read and think about, there was the winding of the watch to be attended to, he kept working at sculpture, and of course he had his practical needs to provide for.

Abel also kept busy taking it easy. Only when taking it easy, he'd learned, could one properly do one's wondering. One night while he was resting under the stars and enjoying the noise of the river and of the November wind, a winged shadow suddenly hung over him, blacking out the stars at which he'd been gazing. Instinct brought him to his feet and sent him diving into a crevice between two rocks.

In mute terror he crouched in the crevice while the owl, with grappling talons, tried to fish him out. It stood on the rock and poked in, while Abel made himself smaller and smaller and receded farther and farther into the seam. Then the poking stopped and the owl scrabbled about on the rock, staring into the night with unfathoming eyes. It took off at last and perched in a tree.

Abel could see the dark shape of the owl in the branches above, and the vibrating stars beyond. Where had this trespasser come from? Why? Had it perhaps seen Abel's signals? He'd been astounded by the stillness with which it had dropped from the sky. There'd been no beat, no ruffle, of wings. This was bone-chilling, to be approached so noiselessly by a winged assassin.

Abel's star was up there among the others. It seemed to say, "I see you both." Abel broke from his sanctuary and dashed for the log. The owl was right behind him. Abel ran as fast as his thin, terrified legs would take him.

He gasped when the owl seized him. He was snatched and rushed aloft, sick with fear, into the ominous air. He had the wit, and just enough strength, to pull out his penknife, open the blade, and frantically slash at the owl's horny toes.

With a screech the owl released him, and Abel fell

with no fear at all of falling. He scrambled with awkward haste to his house, plunged in, and barred the entrance with stones. The next moment he felt the owl land on the hollow log and his innards quivered. Abel crouched motionless in a corner. He could hear the owl shuffle about right above him, a single tail away.

As the night advanced, terror turned to resentment. The mouse considered battling the owl with his knife, putting out his stupid eyes with a pointed pole, setting fire to his feathers with a torch. Indignant and unfearing, he fell asleep.

In the morning, caution returned. He peered from his windows, craning his head upward, and made sure there was no dealer of death on his roof. Most of that day he spent in his bed of milkweed fluff, and ventured out only in the late afternoon, carrying over his shoulder a long pole, his open knife tied to the end.

After his encounter with the owl, he was extremely wary for a long time, even in full daylight, when owls are expected to sleep.

°11°

In late November, Abel was on his way home from the book, mulling over a chapter he had just read. The bears were going to war, against bears from another country. They were going even though, on both sides, everyone wanted peace. This was something to think about, with so much time to think.

The sky was gray. Nature looked its drabbest. Abel thought he saw snowflakes, not falling, just wandering about in the air. Then there were more and he felt a few melt on his head. That winter was coming he had known all along, but here was more evidence and it made him uneasy. Was he as prepared as he ought to be? There was an owl around too, with nasty intentions, and that added to his uneasiness. The environment didn't seem altogether friendly.

In the dead grass he saw a gray-brown feather. Certain that it could only be the owl's, he took it home. There he poked the quill into the soft, rotting wood of his floor, where it stood erect, a sort of talisman. He owned something of the owl's, from his very body, but the owl had nothing of his. This gave him a sense of advantage, at least for the moment.

He found himself uttering an incantation at the
feather, not knowing where the words came from:

> Foul owl, ugly you,
> You'll never get me,
> Whatever you do.
> You cannot hurt me,
> You cannot kill,
> You're in my power,
> I have your quill!

He felt he was casting a spell on the detested bird of prey that would paralyze its evil force. After this, out in his yard in the light, descending snow, Abel addressed Amanda's statue as if it were she herself. "Amanda," he said, "I am safe." Then he went indoors and worked at making himself a winter cape, with hood. He wove two layers of cloth from the fine filaments of grass, and sandwiched in between the two layers some of the milkweed fluff he'd stored in his log.

Still full of forebodings of a hard winter, he foraged about for what he was sure was the last edible stuff on the island: various seeds, dry berries, mushrooms. He crammed his rooms full of these viands. Perhaps it was more than he would need to see the winter through, but he had no way of knowing. Anyway, his abundant store eased his misgivings.

Engrossed one day in these practical chores, he was shocked to see the owl again, up on a branch in a tree near his house. It was asleep, but its erect posture, like that of a sentinel of hell, its eyes, which even shut seemed to stare, the tight grasp of its talons on the bough, and the bloody sunset in the sky behind it, filled poor Abel with wintry dread. He hurried home, his heart tripping. What should he do? Could he possibly kill the obnoxious creature while it slept, so it would die as if in a dream? How? With a rock on the end of a rope? With fire? With a burning javelin of wood?

So many birds had gone south. Why not the owl?

Was an owl really a bird? What an odd, unheavenly bird! Abel, back in his log, knelt in prayer and asked a question he had asked before, though never so urgently: Why did God make owls, snakes, cats, foxes, fleas, and other such loathsome, abominable creatures? He felt there had to be a reason.

°12°

In December, Abel began talking to himself. He had done it before, but only internally. Now he spoke out loud, and the sound of his own voice vibrating in his body felt vital. Addressing himself by name, he would give advice, or ask questions and answer them. Sometimes he argued back and forth, Abel with Abel, and even got quite angry when he disagreed with his own opinions. He often found himself hard to convince.

He talked aloud to Amanda too, addressing her statue. He assured her that he would see her again, and the others he loved. There was no question he'd be getting off the island, though as yet he had no idea how. He was patient; that is, he considered himself patient. Because what other love-longing, wife-craving, home-sick creature would remain so pacingly calm, so nervously resolute, so crazily sane, as long as Abel had?

The first real snowfall was a tail deep. Abel made himself snowshoes and went to his book with a homemade shovel in one arm, his spear in the other. He dug the book out of the snow and read Chapter XIX.

By Chapter XIX, the bear war was at its worst; many had been killed or wounded. It made Abel wonder about civilization. But, come to think of it, the owl, who was not civilized, was pretty warlike too. The hero, Captain Burin, was writing home from the battlefield to the one he had waltzed with in the first chapter, the one he loved. It was also winter in the story, and a drunken sergeant was saying things that were foolish and wise and funny—he wished he were hibernating instead of warring. Some of his statements made Abel roll around on the page, his cloudy breath exploding in spasms of laughter.

It was hard to cover the book when he finished his reading for the day, because the leaves stuck together in frozen sheets. His paws got icy cold. At home, he had to drink some of his wine to dispel the chill in his bones.

On his way home from Chapter XXI, he had a perilous encounter with the owl. But he wasn't caught off guard. Whenever the spear was in his paw, the owl was on his mind, as he, apparently, was always on the mind of the owl. Each one kept a sharp eye out—the would-be killer, and the intended victim.

Hoping to catch Abel napping, the owl swept down from an old decayed tree—it seemed at home in rotten trees—but Abel had his spear at the ready the moment the owl reached him. The owl swerved off as Abel thrust at it, and pretended to fly away defeated, but immediately it swooped down again. This time Abel slashed sideways and thrust viciously upward, and he could feel the point of his knife penetrate the owl's flesh, though the owl made no sound.

It only winced, and fending off the spear with one claw, it ripped off Abel's cape with the other. In a fit of fear and rage, Abel thrust again and again, desperately, without plan. His fury so upset and bewildered the owl that it flew upward and roosted on a dead limb of the tree, staring down in disbelief.

Instead of making off while he had the advantage, Abel cocked his spear and challenged the owl to descend and fight. The owl continued to stare.

"Coward!" Abel screamed, the veins swelling on his neck. "Come down and do battle—bird, reptile, fiend, or whatever kind of villain you are!" If the owl was offended at Abel's insults, it didn't show that it was. Solemnly, it blinked and stared.

"Down with unsightly devils! Down with evil of any sort!" Abel yelled, and with all his might he foolishly flung his spear at the bird of prey. It struck the branch where the owl stood, and fell to the ground. As Abel ran to retrieve his weapon, the owl dived. Abel dodged and raced around the trunk of the tree. The owl couldn't fly in circles any faster than Abel could run, so there was always the tree between them. The chase went on and on, sometimes reversing direction.

This mad carrousel so offended the owl's ancient sense of decorum that it grew confused and crashed into the tree. It had to go off somewhere to sit in a huff, unruffle its feathers, and regain its ruthless composure. Abel grabbed his spear and cape and scampered home.

By now, Abel owned three of the owl's feathers—he was quite sure they were the owl's. Without waiting to catch breath after his heroic skirmish, he began uttering, over these detested feathers, the most horrible imprecations imaginable.

Heaven forfend that the owl should have suffered a fraction of what Abel wished it. Abel wished that its feathers would turn to lead so it could fall on its head from the world's tallest tree, that its beak would rot and become useless even for eating mush, that it should be blind as a bat and fly into a dragon's flaming mouth, that it should sink in quicksand mixed with broken bottles, very slowly, to prolong its suffering, and much more of the same sort.

December grew steadily colder. Abel began tearing margins from the pages of his book and using this paper to fill the chinks in his doorway whenever the stones were set in place. Even so, the cold lanced through, especially when it was windy.

°13°

Abel spent most of January and February, and part of March, indoors. In January there was a great blizzard. The snow descended from the bleary sky in thick, heavy curtains, through a long night. Curled up in his bed, Abel listened despondently to the howling and yowling, the lashing and whistling of the wind.

His log was buried deep, and though a dim light penetrated the snow, almost none got in through the tightly shuttered windows. Even by day, he had to probe his way around. Fortunately, some air filtered through the tightly packed crystals.

Hardly knowing day from night, Abel slept and kept no schedule, and the days came and left, uncounted. His chief occupation when awake was finding his food

in the groping dark of his storerooms and eating it, which was a sort of tiresome ritual, a solemn munching. Otherwise, he yawned, oh how he yawned, turned over time and again, thrashed around, ever so much, scratched, over and over, pushed the shells of acorns, hickory nuts, and sunflower seeds out of his way, and thought of nothing.

Meanwhile, the sun, and occasional thaws, kept lowering the level of the snow, so that eventually Abel had the thrill of seeing the light that had long been denied him slice through the edge of a wind-struck shutter. He woke up one day and there it was—things were visible!

"Abel," he shouted, "do you hear me? I can see!" He flung the shutter open. How beautiful everything looked after the prolonged darkness. How unspeakably beautiful even the shells on the floor. How vividly actual and therefore marvelous!

Abel opened his doorway and let the light flood in. The day seemed confident of its own splendor. The icicles hanging in the open entrance glittered. One was as big as Abel himself. He ate, and drank cold water from a clay pot. Then he shoved the great accumulation of shells out of his house and went to stand before Amanda's statue, which was chest-deep in snow.

"Dear heart, I love you," he exclaimed. "What a lovely day! It's February, isn't it? I need to be moving." He flexed his arms, bent backward and forward, and felt foolish before his wife. He didn't know what to say.

He put on his snowshoes, got his shovel and spear, and went to read his book. Captain Burin had been wounded, he remembered. Was he going to live or not? He was going to live; his wounds were healing, thank God. And spring was coming. The talk of spring filled Abel with unbearable longing. How deeply one felt when alone!

It *was* February, as Abel had surmised, and now winter really took hold. January had been only the prelude. Abel came in from his book one afternoon, unable to keep his body from shaking. His teeth chattered and clacked, and nothing would make his frigid shuddering stop. His snout ran, his eyes teared and grew dim, his head pounded and pained.

It was a time when even the most stalwart of mice would wish to be an infant again in his mother's warm embrace. He tottered about, shivering, and stuffed every open chink as well as he could with his palsied paws, until no light came through anywhere. The only source of warmth was his own heat-hungry body.

How wonderful a fire would be, but if he made one, he realized, he could burn himself out of his home, or anyway use up the oxygen. He donned his entire wardrobe, got all his mats together, all the paper he had torn from the novel, whatever milkweed fluff he could find in his storerooms, and half sitting, half reclining against a wall, he quilted himself all around with these paddings and buried his face in Amanda's scarf. Gradually his shivering subsided and his tired muscles relaxed. He tucked his head under his coverings and his breath helped warm his body.

Thus began another long month of sad sequestration inside the log. Whenever Abel was convinced it couldn't get any colder, it got still colder. The wind tore wildly around the world, whipping up the snow in mountainous drifts, breaking frozen branches off trees, sending icicles clattering to the glassy ground. Abel listened and it lasted so long he stopped hearing it. But still it went on.

He was sick. He was weak; merely to turn over took great effort; and he was wretched. One day he found himself wondering, with dull resentment, why Amanda hadn't tied her scarf on better, so that he wouldn't have had to chase it out of the cave. If she were less dreamy, more attentive to reality, if she had tied her scarf on tighter, he would now, this moment, be at home, wearing his velvet jacket and satin-lined pantofles, ensconced in an easy chair among plump pillows, reading a good book, or perhaps merely looking out his window at the snow. There'd be a fire in the fireplace, lentil soup with an onion in it simmering on the stove, Amanda would be at her escritoire correcting a poem, or better still, she'd be in his lap covering him with warm kisses. The cold and the wind outside would only set off the indoor coziness.

But he wasn't at home, nowhere near it. He thought of his loved ones, his faraway friends. Amanda was his mate, yes, and would always be. His parents, sisters, brothers, and friends would always be his parents, sisters, brothers, and friends, but his feeling for them all had become shadowy. How could he go on having warm, alive feelings for merely remembered beings? Living was more than remembering, imagining. He wanted the

real Amanda at his side, and he tried to reach out to her. His messages, it seemed, could not travel through the icy air.

He became somnolent in his cold cocoon. In his moments of dim-eyed wakefulness he had no idea how much time had passed since he was last awake—whether an hour, a day, or a week. He was cold, but he knew he was as warm as he could get. The water in his clay pot was frozen solid. His mind was frozen. It began to seem it had always been winter and that there was nothing else, just a vague awareness to make note of the fact. The universe was a dreary place, asleep, cold all the way to infinity, and the wind was a separate thing, not part of the winter, but a lost, unloved soul, screaming and moaning and rushing about looking for a place to rest and reckon up its woes.

Somewhere out there, in the night sky—and it could only be night—were the glittering stars, and among them his, the one he had always known. This star, his, millions of miles away, was yet closer than Amanda, because if he had the will and the strength to get up, uncover his window, and look out, he could see it. He knew, therefore, that it existed. But as for Amanda, father, mother, sisters, brothers, aunts, uncles, cousins, friends, and the rest of society and the animal kingdom, he had to believe they were there, and it was hard to have this faith. As far as he really knew, he himself was the only, lonely, living thing that existed, and in his coma of coldness, he was not so sure of that.

·14·

Sometime in March, Abel felt he was thawing out. More wakeful than he'd been, he realized that winter had become less cold, and he bestirred himself to be up and around. He went outside feeling weak, but as he moved about under the wide, blue sky, breathing the clear air and exercising his limbs, he grew stronger.

There were two crocuses in the snow, sure harbingers of spring. Enlivened by this miracle, the dainty flowers braving the cold, he bustled about outside his log, setting things in order. He wound his watch, listened in rapture to its steady ticking, and went to read his book, really more to be back in his old routine than for the sake of reading.

The sun seemed full of plans, less bored with the world than it had been, less aloof. But after a pleasant day, it turned terribly cold again at night, and Abel crawled back under all his coverings, disappointed. Yet the very next morning it was again spring.

Snow melted, revealing the earth. The river, swollen with freshets from the thawing, was swifter than ever, exultantly rushing along. Abel finished reading his book in a few more visits and he was glad to be finished, because what was happening around him was a lot more exciting than any book. Now he liked to lie in the warm sun on the open patches of ground and be part of the

world's awakening.

He visited the birch, sat in his favorite roost, and admired the birch's buds as one admires a friend's babies. At night he found his star in the sky and was happy—in case the star had missed him—to show he was still alive. All this time of burgeoning life and joy, he hadn't failed to carry his spear and watch out for the owl. He never saw it, and concluded that it must have gone away, if it hadn't died during the deadly cold months.

Of course Abel took to communing again with Amanda, and by April he was rather sure they were in touch with each other. By then there were many bright birds about, setting up house in the north after their sea-

son in the south, expressing delight at being back. Fresh grass pushed through the old, dead stubble, buds embroidered the trees. Abel saw his whole world suffused with green.

When the flowers appeared in May, he went crazy. Violets, dandelions, pinks, forget-me-nots bedecked the island. Abel ate grass and young violet greens, fresh food with the juice of life. He drank large draughts of his wine and ran about everywhere like a wild animal, shouting and yodeling. How it would surprise his

family to see him now! A group of geese passed overhead, honking. He waved a greeting. They passed on.
At times he felt he had no need of others.

He bathed in the fresh cold water at the river's edge
and lay on his back under the sun, trying to fathom the
firmament. One day, as he was sunning this way, with
wine in his belly, who should come huffing and puffing
and staggering out of the stream but an obese, elderly
frog. Drunk as he was, Abel wondered if he was seeing
things. But the frog began to talk.

"Ho! Wow! Whoosh! Whoa! Goshamighty! I never thought I'd make it." He flung himself down on the bank, flopped over on his back, legs and arms outstretched, and spluttered some disconnected words.

Overjoyed at hearing civilized speech again, Abel ran over to the recumbent frog and looked down at him, beaming with candid delight.

The frog blinked. "Hi!" he said. "Wow! Did I have a time with that river! And that waterfall! I thought I'd drown!"

"What happened?" asked Abel. The frog sat up. Abel sat down beside him. Having come from the busy world of society, the frog was less surprised to see Abel than Abel was to see him.

"Gower Glackens is the name," said the frog. "Who might you be? Where am I?"

"On an island," Abel answered. "You are talking to Abelard Hassam di Chirico Flint—for short, Abel."

"Pleased to meet you," said Gower, extending a cold, clammy hand. Abel had never enjoyed shaking hands with his frog friends, but he enjoyed grasping Gower's. "Imagine someone my age, with all my years of experience, letting himself get into that kind of water! Spring fever, I guess. I'm always a little batty after lying in the cold mud all winter. The sun made me think I could navigate anything. The river can't handle all those freshets pouring in. It goes wild. Where is this, anyway? Is there a town here? A post office? Any boats?"

"No," said Abel. "There's only me. I'm sorry."

"Don't be sorry," said Gower. "I'd rather find you than find no one. Why are you here?"

"I came the way you did," said Abel, "against my will." And for the next half hour he told his story.

"Wow!" said the frog when Abel was finished. "I was sure I was dead after that waterfall. I must have hit the bottom, filled my big mouth with sand. I didn't know where I was going after that. I just went. Gosh! My family must be worried. They're all asking, Where's Gramps?"

He told about his big family and where he came from. Abel had never heard of the place. And the frog had never heard of Mossville.

"Let's go to my house," Abel said. "It's over that way." He helped Gower to his feet and conducted him back to the log, where he gave him a big drink of wine.

Gower drank in glugging gulps. "I needed that," he said. Then he went into a trance. He squatted on the ground, as frogs do, blinked in what seemed to Abel a smug way, and remained motionless. Abel saw him as crude, but utterly charming.

He prodded him. "Gower?"

"Who? What? Where am I?" said Gower. "Oh, it's you." He did this often, as Abel was to learn.

·15·

They remained together till June and became fast friends. Gower said he would be leaving as soon as he regained his strength and the swiftness of the stream had sufficiently subsided. "I wish I could carry you off the island," he told Abel, "but I'll have enough trouble making it by myself. I'm not what I was in my mating days."

"You could carry a rope across for me," Abel said, and he outlined his original plan for a rope bridge.

"That doesn't make sense," said Gower. "Do you realize how far down the river I'll be when I hit the other side? That rope would have to be thousands of lily pads long. Having it attached to me, maybe catching on things and all, could give me a heart attack. I'm no tadpole, you know!"

"But you *will* come back with rescuers, won't you?" Abel asked.

"Sure as shooting," said Gower. "That'll be the first order of business."

"And you *will* get in touch with my wife, won't you? I'll give you her address."

"Wife?" said Gower.

"I've told you about her many times," said Abel. "That's her statue."

"Oh, yes," said Gower. "Of course. I remember." He was always forgetting things.

One day Abel started on a statue of his new friend. As he shaped the clay, they conversed. Abel learned that Gower played bass fiddle in a small orchestra whose specialty was country music, had great-grandchildren by the dozen, all of whom were musical, and was happy with his old wife, though they often quarreled and spent whole days sitting around in a huff, trying to remember what they were angry about.

Once Gower asked Abel what his trade or profession was. "I haven't found my vocation yet," Abel answered. "The only real work I've ever done has been here on this island."

"Holy bloater! What did you live on?" Gower wanted to know.

"My mother has provided for me," Abel answered. "I'm quite well off."

Gower grinned. "You sure don't look it," he commented, surveying Abel's frayed trousers and stained, tattered shirt.

"I usually dress better than this," said Abel, laughing. For a moment he was embarrassed, but then he wiped the clay off his paws with the tail of his shirt.

Abel talked about Amanda, about her poetry, her grace, her tendency to dream. He speculated on why *her* movements, *her* gestures, *her* voice, *her* way of dressing, were so much more charming and heart-winning than those of any other female mouse he had ever known, including his own dear mother and favorite sister. It puzzled him.

"It's the magic of love," burped Gower.

"Could you raise your chin a bit higher?" Abel asked.

Gower did not move. He was in one of his reptilian torpors again. There he crouched with heavy-lidded, unseeing eyes, not asleep, not awake, not dead, not alive, still as a stone, gyrating with the world.

Abel watched in wonder. Gower's eyelids lifted slightly and his tongue suddenly shot forward and nailed a fly, which he swallowed. This feat always impressed Abel, and disgusted him too.

"Could you raise your head a trifle?" he asked again.

It took a week to complete the statue. It was the best Abel had ever done, a perfect representation of stupefied repose. Every wart was lovingly modeled; the eyes bulged properly, the full throat with the delicate wrinkles of age was definitely Gower's. The fulsome belly, the haunches and feet, rested firmly on the ground. There was a vague smile on the broad mouth and in the lines of the closed eyelids that made the frog appear to be meditating on a homey universe.

Abel was so proud of his accomplishment he wished he could show it to Amanda that minute. "Well, what do you think of it?" he asked Gower.

"It's me all right," Gower said. "It's more me than what I see in the mirror. It's what I see when I imagine how I look. It's a work of art, that's what it is!"

Abel allowed the compliment to stand. Looking at his own opus, he saw no reason to pretend modesty.

"I think you've found your vocation," opined Gower.

Abel swallowed, then blushed. He had never thought along these lines.

°16°

Early one morning in the middle of June, Abel heard a knocking on his log and stepped outside. It was Gower, who'd been sleeping by the river. His manner seemed less than casual.

"What's up?" Abel inquired.

"I've been watching the water," said the frog. "It's not as rushy as it was." Actually, the river had returned to normal a week earlier, but Gower had been unusually meditative lately. "I think I can make it to the other side."

"Why so soon?" Abel asked, full of sudden foreboding. "We're just getting to know one another. Aren't you happy here? Have I offended you in any way?"

"I'm happy, all right," Gower glumped. "But I'm worried. I've been thinking of Gammer, my wife, and all the children, and their children and their children's children. They can't be getting on too well without me."

"How I hate to see you go," sighed Abel.

"I hate to go," allowed Gower.

"Then don't," said Abel.

"My family," said Gower.

"*I'm* your family," said Abel.

Gower's eyes bulged. "You're a mouse," he said.

"How about some breakfast?" asked Abel.

"No, thanks," said Gower. "I've been eating flies all morning. They're at their best today."

"You won't forget to come back with help, will you?" Abel pleaded. "And you will get in touch with Amanda? 89 Bank Street, Mossville."

"Don't worry," said Gower.

"Don't forget," said Abel.

"How could I?" said Gower. "It's the first thing I'll do after I get home and see my family." Then he went into his trance; his eyes rolled up under the lids as if he were storing a memory there for future use.

When his absent mind returned, they walked down to the water, both sad to be parting. "Knowing you, dear Gower, has been one of the most rewarding experiences of my life," said Abel.

"Ditto," said Gower. "Shucks, why grieve? It's only temporary. That's a great statue you made of me. It will be in a museum someday, I'll bet."

"Thank you," said Abel.

"I'll have to play my bull fiddle for you when we meet again."

"We *will* meet again, won't we?" said Abel. "You won't forget?"

"You bet," said Gower. He was standing on the bank of the river with bowed legs. "Farewell, my friend." He put a cold hand on Abel's shoulder.

"Farewell, good Gower," said Abel in a husky voice.

Gower dived. He disappeared under the water and in a while his head bobbed up, far out and downstream. He waved back with his webbed hand. Abel waved. And then Gower was off and swimming, a strong breast stroke, making lateral headway but also being carried downstream, until he disappeared, at least from sight.

Abel was certain the frog would make the other bank. He wished he could swim as well. He watched the empty river for a while, then walked back to his log in tears. He sat on a stone, looking with wet eyes at a blurred world at the statues, Amanda, Gower, and the others, at the daisies beyond the statues, at the tall, silent trees. He could not stand his own sorrow.

The watch ticked away without feeling. Abel got up, went to the cherry birch, and climbed up to his roost. He sat there all day, not thinking, numb.

At night his star appeared. "I'm lonesome," Abel said when he saw it.

"So am I," the star seemed to answer.

°17°

Summer progressed. While waiting for Gower Glackens's rescue crew, Abel kept busy, providing for himself, working at his art, doing whatever he could to be steadily occupied. He ate dandelion greens, birch bark, pigweed, wild onions, mushrooms, grass seed, watercress. He found he liked burdock root very much, and when the strawberries turned red, he had them on his breath all day.

He began to make sculptures of plants, and the more elaborate he made them, the more it distracted his mind. He took to drawing, with bits of charcoal, in the empty spaces on the pages of his bear novel, and he discovered he could color his drawings by rubbing them with flower petals.

He swam. He went on long, rambling walks. He kept his watch ticking. But all the time he never forgot he was waiting, waiting for his rescuers. Either Gower would bring them, or Amanda, or both. He waited for weeks. No one came.

Finally, he was achingly certain that Gower had forgotten him. He had surely succeeded in crossing the river, but somewhere along the watery way his memory of a mouse named Abel had leached out.

Abel looked at Gower's statue and had new insight into the mystical expression on his face. He realized that

if Gower was not drilled into remembering the everyday world, it became a dream that faded from mind as he dwelled on the ultimate reality beyond it. If he remembered his family, that was because a family is the one thing nobody can ever forget. Abel built fires to make smoke signals again and sent messages down the river on scraps from his book.

In the hugging heat of July he was struck with a new, most exciting possibility. For weeks it hadn't rained and the river looked a bit slower, a mite shallower. Could he, could he possibly, hope that the short dry spell would continue into a drawn-out drought? That the river would get low enough for him to risk swimming across? He would hope it, but he warned himself not to be too devastated if it didn't happen.

He climbed his cherry birch. He was still wearing Amanda's scarf. It was the only thing he wore that was not in shreds. He had had to discard his shoes and socks sometime ago. His necktie had been used to help hold up his hammock. He removed the scarf from his neck and let the birch feel its wispy softness. Then he fell to kissing it.

He had avoided dwelling too much on Amanda, even while waiting for rescuers. Now she occupied his mind constantly. He could see her beautiful black eyes vividly. Dreaminess and vivacity, what a wonderful combination of qualities! How much her brisk, graceful bustling had enlivened his idle days! How often, when he'd been lying on the sofa at home, wondering what to make of his life, her mere passing through the room had cheered him up. Even her scoldings he remembered with pleasure. She had only meant him well. His whole being ached to be with her.

He was glad the sun was so fierce and burning. He slept on the ground outside his log and was happy to wake every morning to a bright, torrid day. The first thing he did on waking was to look at the river. Its flow was clearly diminished. A few sand bars had become visible, and dry rocks showed that had previously been under water.

The island was still green in spite of the drought, and it was green on the opposite shores of the river. But, beyond, the green looked tarnished and the tops of the distant wooded hills were turning brown. That dying vegetation gladdened Abel's heart.

He woke one morning in August to find the sky dark with clouds. A few drops of rain had fallen and been quickly absorbed by the dry ground. Abel ran to the river and looked up and down its length. It's now or never, he decided.

He raced back to his yard and, addressing himself to Amanda's statue, declared, "I'm coming home!" Then, entering his log, he looked around as if to etch forever

in his memory this piece of dead tree that had been his haven. He lovingly caressed each of his sculptures. The ticking watch urged him not to tarry. He ran to the birch and pressed his face to its bark. The birch stood erect and encouraging.

He hurried to the river, to the tip of a small peninsula. For one moment he turned to stare back and was filled with sudden anguish. The island had been his home for a full year. It had given him sustenance, guidance, warmth, like a parent. Something important had happened there. How could he help loving it!

"Goodbye," he said. "I'll be back." And he waded into the water.

·18·

When the water was neck-high, Abel flung himself forward and started swimming. He was carried downstream, but he made progress across too. It was still, for him, a strong current, but not like before. He swam with great resolve. He didn't mind the water engulfing him now and then, filling and hurting his nostrils. He snorted bravely when it did. He was at last actually doing what for weeks he had been doing only in his imagination.

Fortunately, he was able to climb a rock after a while and rest there until his panting had subsided. He was a quarter of the way over! Now he confronted the most challenging, the deepest, part of the stream. He had to believe he would be able to reach another rock to rest on. Having come so far, he felt his confidence swell. He was wiry-strong after his rugged year in the wilds. The Abel who was leaving was in better fettle, in all ways, than the Abel who had arrived in a hurricane, desperately clinging to a nail.

He sucked his lungs full of air and threw himself into the water. Again he was carried downstream and again made crossways progress, stroking and kicking with power. He felt a minnow brush his leg and he exulted to be doing so well in the minnow's own medium. He kept swimming. But soon he was overwhelmed by the water's swiftness. It tore and tumbled and he was swung

around like someone dragged against his will into a reckless dance.

He stopped swimming, lay with his arms and legs outstretched, face to the heavens, and let himself be carried along for a while. With a sodden thump, he again found a rock. Blessed rock. He mounted it and rested on his back, his body heaving. It was very much as he had imagined it would be—difficult. But he was mastering the river, and he felt he was being guided. Hallelujah! Light rain began to fall. It didn't matter. Abel knew he was equal to the rest of his task. He dived once more. A dozen strokes and his feet were touching bottom! He was on a gravelly welt of raised river bed. He walked across it and, without hesitating, made his final, easy swim.

When at last he came out of the water and touched the shore he had been yearning toward for the whole round of a passing year, he experienced a burst of astounding joy. He lay on the longed-for ground, flooded with ecstatic feelings of triumph and well-being. Then he broke into uncontrollable laughter. He was a free mouse!

In a while he started upstream, walking along the bank, where no tall grass obstructed the way. His thoughts were full of the future, but they were also full of the past. He was imagining ahead to Amanda, and beyond her to his family, his friends, and a renewed life in society that would include productive work, his art;

but he was also remembering his year on the island, a unique and separate segment of his life that he was now glad he had gone through, though he was also glad it was over.

As to what was to come, he began to be disturbed by vague apprehensions. What was he really walking toward? Would Amanda be home? Had things changed during his year of exile? What if, believing him dead, she had married another? Many mice had been in love with her. Was she even alive? He had been in touch with her, but had he really been in touch? Or had he only imagined it?

After much walking, he arrived at a spot opposite his island. He saw it for the first time from a far perspective,

embracing its wholeness. No wonder he loved it; it was beautiful. Through the rain he saw his beloved birch and all the trees around it. These images would be his forever.

Having no wish to dally, he continued steadily northward. When he climbed the steep hill alongside the waterfall, he was amazed that he had traveled over this cataract when it was much mightier, and had survived. He had been through great ordeals, but here he was. Life surely meant him well. He kept walking.

If only the rain would end, if only for an hour. He felt the need to be dry. Eventually, he found shelter in a natural vault of jutting rock, lay down, and was instantly asleep.

When he woke, the moon was out and a cat was staring him in the face.

°19°

For a moment Abel was stiff with terror, then he scrambled to his feet, but before he could get away he was in the cat's mouth. He could feel her sharp teeth holding him firmly by the skin of his back

Now he was being trotted off somewhere in a very businesslike way, and there was no question about the nature of the business. His thoughts remained remarkably clear. Was this the culmination of all his plans, all

his yearning, all his work, all his waiting, for a long, long year? Would he *not* see Amanda again? His family? Not be at home again? Not be? Could life be so cruel?

The cat dropped him on the ground. He darted off like an arrow. The cat pounced, held him under a paw, and in another moment let go. Abel did nothing. He couldn't tell whether it was fear that held him, or sudden loss of hope, or whether he was playing dead out of long-forgotten instinct. It amounted to the same thing. He was motionless. The cat was motionless. They waited.

Then, swipe! She struck him, tossing him into the air with a cuff of her paw. At that, Abel was off and running, the cat after him. Again she snagged him in her teeth and again she let him go. Abel crouched, only his eyes moving. He was bleeding, yet he felt strangely detached now, curious about what the cat, or he himself, would do next.

The cat watched. She blinked. Was she bored? Abel felt she was being much too casual about his imminent end, as though it were only one of many she had contrived. He saw a tree a short way off and scampered wildly toward it. The cat allowed him a head start, perhaps to add interest to the chase. Abel fled up the tree in sudden streaks, going this way, that, under and over branches, around the trunk. The cat stayed close, but slipped once, while Abel kept going.

He made his wild way to the very top, to the slenderest branch that would support his weight. The cat couldn't follow that far. They rested. They could see each other

clearly in the moon's mellow light. Looking down from the safety of his position, Abel realized that the cat had to do what she did. She was being a cat. It was up to him to be the mouse.

And he was playing his part very well. A little smugness crept into his attitude. He seemed to be saying, "It's your move." Whether in response to this, or merely because she was tired of waiting, the cat leaped. Abel gripped his twig. It bent like a bow when she struck it, swung back, swayed, and shook in his grasp, and he could hear the cat drop, hitting branches as she fell, yowling and screaming in pain and amazement. He heard the thud as she struck the ground, and her crazy caterwauling as she shot off in utter confusion. The unruffled moon continued to shine.

Abel stayed in the tree and eventually slept. In the light of morning, taking his bearings, he was overjoyed to see Mt. Eunice to the northwest. The fire observatory was on the side visible to him, and at last he knew where he was. He had to travel northward with a bias to the east, and he would be in Mossville sooner or later—with luck, in less than a day. He would be seeing *her* again! He hustled down the tree and started homeward, half walking, half running.

·20·

By late afternoon he was on rocky ground cleft with ravines. It must have been one of these he was flushed down a year ago in the hurricane, because he arrived before long at the cliff with the cave where he and Amanda had taken shelter that day. He pressed on.

He was walking in the woods where he had picnicked with his wife. There were signs of last year's great storm. Broken branches lay on the ground, and uprooted trees with slabs of earth still attached to their bases. In the shade of the woods it was still quite green in spite of the drought.

Abel's heart pounded with his exertions and excitement. And with dreadful anxiety. Would Amanda be there, at home? Would she be happy to see him? At moments he was afraid he might even be unwelcome. It grew dark and he was glad of it. He had every reason to be in rags, but he didn't want to be seen that way. He didn't want to be seen in any way, not by anyone but Amanda. Later there would be time to see mother, father, family, and all the others.

He reached the edge of town at night. He was in Grover Park. The soft gas lamps were lighted. It was a hot night, and the park was full of townsfolk, outdoors after dinner to keep cool, strolling on the graveled walks, chatting on the benches, laughing, watching the children romp and frisk about. How wonderful, after the year alone in the woods, to see this model of civilized society, the town where he was born. He recognized many faces; he was back where he belonged. But he stayed in the shadows to avoid being seen.

Then, suddenly, whom should he see! She, herself, Amanda! Sitting on a stone bench in a perfectly everyday way.

How could he keep from rushing out and holding her dearness in his arms? He managed to restrain himself. There were others on the bench and on the walk. He had waited a year; he could wait a bit longer. Their reunion should be theirs alone. He hurried quietly home, avoiding any encounter.

Home! He grasped the graceful railing and bounded up the steps. He still had the keys in his ragged pants. He opened the door. It was all exactly as he had left it,

as he had remembered it so often during his exile. It was nothing like his hollow log.

Amanda's radiance was there. How good to see her things about. And his own—his books, his favorite chair. He went into the kitchen, looked in a pot on the stove, tasted the soup.

In the bedroom he looked around with anxious joy at the familiar objects. He washed, with scented soap. He donned his best silk shirt, his purple cravat, his brown velvet jacket with the braided lapels. These elegant clothes felt uncomfortable.

Now, smiling, he put Amanda's scarf on the taboret in the entrance hall where she could see it when she entered, then went into the parlor and lay down on the

plush sofa, his paws behind his head, his heart full of bold expectations. It seemed a long time before Amanda came home. At last he heard the door open and then a gasp and a cry.

"Abel! Oh, dear Abel! It's you! It's really, really you!" Amanda came rushing in and flung herself into Abel's arms. They covered each other with kisses.

When he was able to speak, Abel said, "I've brought you back your scarf."

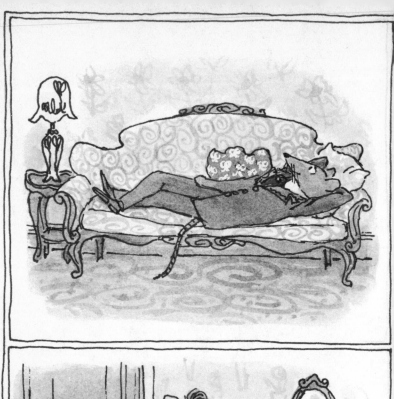